BANCROFT SCHOOL

THE MAGIC NUTCRACKER

A Follett JUST Beginning-To-Read Book

THE
MAGIC NUTCRACKER

Margaret Hillert

Illustrated by Portia Iversen

FOLLETT PUBLISHING COMPANY
Chicago

Library of Congress Cataloging in Publication Data

Hillert, Margaret.
  The magic nutcracker.

  (Follett just beginning-to-read books)
  SUMMARY: When a young girl rescues her nutcracker from an attack by mice, the nutcracker becomes a prince and takes her to see the Snow King and Queen, the Sugar Plum Fairy, and waltzing flowers.
  [1. Fairy tales] I. Iversen, Portia. II. Title.
PZ8.H5425Mag   [E]   80–13667
ISBN 0–695–41456–9 (lib. bdg.)
ISBN 0–695–31456–4 (pbk.)

Library of Congress Catalog Card Number: 80–13667

International Standard Book Number: 0–695–41456–9 Library binding
                                     0–695–31456–4 Paper binding

Third Printing

Is this for me?
It looks like a little man.
What is it for?

Oh, I see.
I can make it work.
And I will have something
good to eat.

6

Now I have to go.
I like you, little man,
but you can not come with me.

Oh, my. Oh, my.
I want my little man.
I will get up and
go look for it.

Oh, oh, oh.
What is this?
What is this?
I do not like it.

11

My little man is down.
This is not good.
How can I help?

Go away.
Go away.
See what I can do
to you.

O - o - o - h!
How did you do that?
You are not little now.
You are a big man.

Yes, I am big now.

And I like you.

I want you to go with me.

I want you to see something.

Now come with me.
Get into this.
It will take us away.

Look at this.

Oh, look at this.

See how pretty it is.

And look who is here.
Guess who.
Can you guess who it is?

Away we go.

Away, away.

What will we find out here?

Here is a girl.

A pretty, pretty girl.

She wants us to come in.

See what she can do.
She is good at it.
We can do it, too.

Oh, my. Oh, my.
Look at this
     and this
          and this!

We can eat it.
It is good, good, good.
Oh, I like it here!

And what have we here?
Something pretty.
Red, yellow, blue.

Come now.
Come with me.
We have to go.
Away, away we go.

Here you are.
Get in. Get in.
I have to go now.

This is funny.
How did I get here?
And how did you get here?
Now you are little.
That is good.
I like you this way.

Margaret Hillert, author of many Follett JUST Beginning-To-Read Books, has been a first-grade teacher in Royal Oak, Michigan, since 1948.

The Magic Nutcracker uses the 66 words listed below.

a	get	make	up
am	girl	man	us
and	go	me	
are	good	my	want(s)
at	guess		way
away		not	we
	have	now	what
big	help		who
blue	here	oh	will
but	how	out	with
			work
can	I	pretty	
come	in		yellow
	into	red	yes
did	is		you
do	it	see	
down		she	
	like	something	
eat	little		
	look(s)	take	
find		that	
for		this	
funny		to	
		too	

BANCROFT SCHOOL